bratz™

Novelization of the Film

By Christine Peymani

With dazzlin' pictures from the movie!

©2007 TM & © MGA Entertainment, Inc.
All Rights Reserved.
Modern Publishing
A Division of Unisystems, Inc.
New York, New York 10022
Printed in the U.S.A.

bratz

Novelization of the Film

www.bratz.com

TM and ©MGA Entertainment, Inc. "Bratz" and all related logos, names, characters, and distinctive likenesses are the exclusive property of MGA Entertainment, Inc. All Rights Reserved. Used under license by Modern Publishing.
16300 Roscoe Boulevard
Van Nuys, CA 91406
(800) 222-4685

Modern Publishing
A Division of Unisystems, Inc.
New York, New York 10022

Printed in the U.S.A.

Chapter 1

Riiing! Yasmin leapt out of bed, tearing off her satin eye mask as she fumbled for the off button on her purple alarm clock. "Seven a.m. already?" she groaned, but then she remembered: Today was her first day at Carry Nation High School, and she and her best friends were ready to take the school by storm!

She flipped on her iPod speaker dock, and one of her favorite pop tunes blared out. Energized by the music, she started singing along, dancing her way over to her computer, where she clicked open a four-way video chat with her best friends Cloe, Jade, and Sasha.

"Morning, ladies!" Cloe trilled, smiling out of the computer screen.

"Are you ready, Chicas?" Yasmin asked.

"Yeah!" her friends chorused.

"Okay. On three," Yasmin declared, and the girls counted down together, "One, two, three!" The girls all whirled to fling open their closets, their movements perfectly synchronized.

Yasmin's closet was crammed full of brightly colored, ethnic-inspired clothing. Sasha's was huge, with racks of clothes as far as the eye can see, and when she presses a button, the motorized racks rotate, revealing even more fabulous threads. Cloe's was stuffed with sports equipment, her skirts and tops poking out from among a jumbled pile of basketballs, soccer balls, hockey sticks, and team jerseys. Jade's was small, neat, and perfectly organized, lined with sensible plaid skirts, modest white blouses, and plain turtleneck sweaters.

"Can you believe it's our first day of high school already?" Yasmin cried.

"I'm so ready for this," Sasha declared. "We're going to be the most fabulous foursome to ever hit the hallways of Carry Nation High."

"So what are we gonna wear?" Cloe asked.

"Hmm…" Sasha flipped through row upon row of clothing. "Aw, man. That new skirt I bought yesterday is at my mom's house." The girls had gone on a marathon shopping spree together the day before to pick out cute new outfits that would be perfect for their first day of high school.

"I thought you were at your mom's house," Jade interrupted.

"Nope," Sasha replied. "I'm at my dad's on Mondays. Joint custody—what can I say?"

"That must be a pain," Jade said sympathetically, but Sasha just shrugged.

"Hey, where's that turquoise shirt I bought?" Yasmin wondered, shoving clothes to the side as she searched for her new purchase.

Cloe pulled the shirt out of her closet and held it up to the camera on her computer. "Sorry, I grabbed your bag by mistake." She paused, then asked, "Do you mind if I wear it?"

"Go for it!" Yasmin told her.

"Thanks!" Cloe replied. "Okay, so how about this turquoise thermal with a tank top and striped warmers?"

"Super-cute!" Yasmin agreed.

"How about this?" Sasha interrupted, holding up a pile of clothes. "Shorts, V-neck top, and leopard-print sneakers."

"Perfect!" Jade replied, then sighed. "And for me, yet another plaid skirt and lame sweater."

"Jade!" Yasmin protested. "We have to make an awesome first impression. Is that really the impression you want to make?"

"You know it isn't," Jade told her, "but it's the impression my parents insist on. Don't worry though-it's just till I get out of the house."

"And then?" Sasha prodded her.

"And then I'm gonna blow y'all away!" Jade declared. She pulled aside a secret panel in the back of her closet to reveal a dazzling array of stylish outfits hidden away back there.

"I guess none of you want to know what *I'm* gonna wear." Yasmin put her hands on her hips, feigning annoyance.

"All we need to know is you'll look fabulous," Sasha said.

"And your shoes will be to die for!" Cloe added.

"Lucky guess," Yasmin said with a grin. She was known for her glamorous style and her shoe addiction, so she knew she shouldn't be surprised that her friends had figured out what look she would pick for such a big day. "Okay, ladies, meet at the front entrance in forty minutes. We'll go in together."

"See you there!" Cloe exclaimed.

"Sayonara!" Jade called with a little wave at the computer screen.

"Ciao, my sisters!" Sasha replied, then closed out her chat window.

Yasmin turned away from the now-blank screen and dashed for the bathroom—she only had forty minutes to get ready, and she still had so much to do.

But when she reached the bathroom, she stopped short at the closed white door. She knocked on the door, and her twelve-year-old brother Manny yelled back, "Wait your turn!"

"Move it, Manny!" she shouted, pounding on the door. "You have ten seconds to get out of there, or I'll tell Mom how much you spent on all those hair products!"

Manny struck a pose in front of the bathroom mirror, running a hand through his wavy brown hair. His hair products covered the bathroom counter, and he began putting the lids back on each of them as he admired his reflection. "Perfection takes time," he said with a satisfied nod, "and I am worth every second!"

He pulled his cell phone out of the pocket of his baggy pants and was about to snap a picture of himself as he flung open the door. But before he could get the shot, Yasmin sashayed past on her way into the bathroom and ruffled his hair playfully. "Lookin' good, Lil' Bro," she teased.

"Nooo! My hair!" Manny wailed. Yasmin smiled at him sweetly as she shut the door behind her and got down to some serious primping.

Twenty minutes later, Yasmin was showered and dressed, her hair and makeup perfect, and she was ready for some breakfast. She peeked into Manny's bedroom, where he was sulking, his carefully groomed hair still sticking up in every direction.

"Lookin' good, Bro," she teased, and he ran straight after her, chasing her down the stairs and into the kitchen. They burst into the crowded kitchen, where their grandma, Bubbie, was scrambling eggs, surrounded by fifteen members of their extended family.

"Hurry up, Niños," Bubbie said. "You don't want to be late." She started to hand each of them a plate loaded with eggs and French toast, but then she noticed Manny's hair. "Manny, go comb your hair—you can't leave the house like that!"

"Ugh!" Manny wailed, running back upstairs.

Bubbie and Yasmin shared a grin. "Come here for a minute," Bubbie whispered, pulling her granddaughter aside. She pulled a wrinkled paper bag out of the pantry and handed it to Yasmin, glancing around to make sure none of the aunts, uncles, or cousins noticed.

Yasmin opened the bag, peered inside,

and squealed with excitement. Turning her back to the rest of the room to hide the bag from view, she pulled out a pair of gorgeous high-heeled purple boots.

"Bubbie, they're fabulous!" she gasped, running upstairs to put them on.

*   *   *

Sasha stood in her kitchen, trying to get the lever on the toaster to stay down. "Dad, the toaster's broken again," she complained. She bit into a piece of toast she'd made earlier while her dad fiddled with the toaster.

"I've got to replace this thing," he said. The doorbell rang, and he told her, "There's your mom. Oh, and remember to tell her that she has to take you to the dentist on Thursday."

"Okay," Sasha agreed. She ran to the front door and threw it open to find her mom, in a suit, standing on the porch. "Hey, Mom!" She gave her mom a quick kiss on the cheek, and added, "I'll be ready in a minute."

"Sounds good," her mom replied. "Oh, and remind your father that he has to take you to the dentist on Thursday."

"Oh, come on," Sasha moaned. "Why can't the two of you just talk to each other? I'm the kid—you're supposed to be the adults."

Sasha ran upstairs just as her dad emerged from the kitchen. He stopped short when he saw his ex-wife standing in the doorway.

They just stared at each other for a moment before Sasha's mom called, "Honey, I'll just wait in the car," and walked out of the house, leaving her ex-husband to stare at the door she'd slammed shut behind her.

*   *   *

Cloe's mom, Katie, was busily cooking with giant canisters of flour and sugar open on the counter and pots, pans, cake molds and cookie trays spread out around her.

Cloe wandered in, still wearing her pink flannel pajamas.

"Good morning, Sweetheart," Katie called. "Can you believe it's your first day of high school? Oh, you're going to have so much fun! Aren't you excited?"

"Excited…and nervous," Cloe admitted.

"Trust me—it'll be wonderful," Katie assured her daughter.

"Mom, everything smells amazing in here," Cloe sighed, breathing in the sweet scent of baked goods. "Yum! What time did you get up to do all this?"

"I never went to bed," Katie told her. "Now come on, Clo-poke. Get a move on! You can't be late for your first day of school. I'll go warm up the van while you get dressed."

"That's okay, Mom," Cloe protested. "I like taking the bus. It gives me time to think."

"Are you sure?" Katie asked. "It's really no problem. The muffins will wait."

"Mom, it's fine," Cloe insisted.

"Okay," Katie agreed with a worried glance at the oven timer. "But here, take this." She reached into her purse and pulled out a tattered ten-dollar bill.

"Thanks, Mom, but I packed a lunch," Cloe replied. "I don't need any cash."

"Please take it." Katie looked at her daughter pleadingly, her eyes wide and tired. "It'll make me feel better."

Cloe saw how important it was to her mom, so she replied, "Okay. Thanks, Mom." She scooted around the kitchen counter and gave her mom a huge hug.

Katie went back to mixing ingredients, and Cloe hurried out of the kitchen, pausing to slip the ten back into her mom's purse while Katie's back was turned.

Chapter 2

Jade's parents pulled up in front of Carry Nation High School in a silver sedan, and Jade hopped out of the back, looking prim and proper in a knee-length skirt and sweater set.

"Bye Mom, bye Dad," Jade called with a wave.

"Wait a second, Jade," her mom said. She stepped out of the car and adjusted Jade's cardigan. "There. Now you look perfect."

Jade's dad, a professional-looking businessman in a button-down shirt and slacks, handed his daughter a neatly printed schedule. "I wanted to make sure you could keep track of everything," he explained, and she smiled at him.

"Jade, remember you have Mathletes, Science Club, Kumon, and violin today," her mother told her, pointing to the schedule.

"Okay, but first I have my first day of school, remember?" Jade replied. "And I better get going!"

"Just let Daddy take a picture first," her mother said, pulling out a small silver camera and posing with her daughter, leaning against Jade's shoulder. "Now one of just her," her mom insisted.

Jade rolled her eyes as flocks of students walked by, snickering at this parental display. "I really better get in there!" Jade declared after her dad snapped a few more shots.

"Have fun today!" her mom called after her as Jade dashed toward the front entrance, where Yasmin and Sasha were already waiting for her.

"Where's Cloe?" Jade asked. Just then, they heard a crash behind them, and turned to see Cloe getting up, a pile of bikes scattered around her.

"There she is," Yasmin said.

"Hi guys!" Cloe cried, brushing herself off. The girls headed over to help her set the trash cans back up, and then Yasmin pulled her three best friends into a huddle.

"Okay. It's our first day in a big school, and we're only freshmen," Yasmin began. "But what are we going to do?"

"Blend?" Cloe suggested, and Jade elbowed her.

"Own it!" Sasha declared.

"Right!" Yasmin agreed. Her best friends cheered and gave each other high fives as they broke out of their huddle, then surveyed their new domain.

"Um, guys?" Jade reminded them, looking out of place in her bland skirt and sweater set.

"Oops," Yasmin replied. "Re-huddle!"

The girls closed in around Jade, providing cover while she yanked off her parent-approved clothing to reveal an amazing outfit of her own design underneath. While she changed, her friends kept talking about their plans for the year.

"So this year, I'm definitely gonna *own* Carry Nation cheerleading," Sasha announced.

"I'll try out for soccer," Cloe said timidly.

"And you'll be the star of the team!" Sasha insisted.

"The team would be lucky to have you," Jade chimed in.

"Thanks, guys," Cloe replied. "But I'm seriously nervous. I mean, the high school team is really good."

"And so are you," Sasha said. "No one drops a kick like you! By the end of this year, everyone will wanna 'bend it like Cloe.'"

Cloe smiled shyly at her friends. "I hope so. I just feel like filmmaking is my calling, but everyone says soccer is my thing, so I guess that's what I should go for."

"You should definitely follow your dreams," Yasmin told her, "but you are an *amazing* soccer player, so it seems like a shame to let it go to waste."

"Thanks, Yas," Cloe replied. "So, what are your big dreams for this year?"

"I don't know yet," Yasmin admitted. "I might join the newspaper—you know I love writing."

"Yas, you have to join choir—you know you have the most amazing voice ever!" Sasha told her.

"Not a chance," Yasmin replied, blushing. "You know I can't sing in front of people."

"But in choir you won't have to sing alone," Cloe pointed out. "So that should be way less scary, right?"

"Cloe, remember Kindergarten?" Yasmin asked. "Me, 'Mary Had a Little Lamb,' throw up, thirty screaming kids? Yeah, I think I'll go for journalism instead."

"Come on, Yas," Cloe continued, shoving

her friend playfully, but Jade interrupted their banter.

"*I'm* gonna own the science club," she declared. Her friends all turned to stare at her.

"Sure, work that high IQ, but don't forget your passion for fashion," Sasha said.

"It's just to keep Mom and Dad off my back," Jade explained. "I'm also gonna own Home-Ec."

"That's not exactly the kind of girl-power goal we had in mind," Sasha protested.

"Actually, it is," Jade replied. "See, Home-Ec is where the sewing machines are. And I'm gonna need sewing machines to become a totally hot fashion designer."

"Good point," Yasmin agreed.

"Okay, I'm good," Jade announced.

The girls broke their huddle again and checked out Jade's new threads. "Wow," Cloe said.

"I designed it myself," Jade explained. She carefully folded her parent-approved outfit and slipped it into her bookbag.

"Of course you did," Cloe replied with a grin.

"Okay, girls, let's get in there," Yasmin exclaimed. The girls linked arms and headed toward the front door of their new high school.

*   *   *

On the front lawn of the school, a trio of girls in pastel cashmere sweaters sat behind a table draped with a banner reading "Mandatory Freshmen Check-In."

Meredith, the head of this clique, flipped her carefully curled hair over her shoulder and held out a seating chart to her friends, Avery and Quinn.

"Now, being at the top of the social pyramid comes with a lot of responsibility," Meredith explained.

A cute jock strolled by in his football uniform, and Avery and Quinn turned to watch him pass, batting their eyelashes at him.

"Avery! Quinn! Pay attention," Meredith demanded. "I need you to become very familiar with the lunch table seating chart. As you can see, there are forty-eight distinct cliques. Let me break it down for you." She spread the chart across the table, and her friends leaned in to check it out. "You've got the Goths, the skaters, the rockers, and the blingers," she began, pointing out each spot on her map of the quad. "Then over here are the cheerleaders, the girl jocks, the nerds, the hippies, the science geeks, and the trendsetters. And you've got the drama kids, the preps, and the over-achievers..."

The next kid in a long line that stretched across the lawn slunk over to the table. Meredith's dog, Paris, perched on the edge of the table in a baby blue sweater that exactly matched her owner's, yipped at the boy as he approached.

"Oh, hi there, little freshman," Meredith cooed, a fake smile plastered across her face. "I'm Meredith, and I'll be helping you find your way. So, let's get started." She looked the boy up and down, taking in his black T-shirt and rumpled jeans, his disheveled hair and the blank expression on his face. "Are you in any clubs?"

"Nope," the kid replied.

"Do you have any interests?" she continued.

"Not really," he said.

"Friends?"

"Nah," he told her.

"Okay, then!" Meredith turned to her friends and announced, "Loner." She pointed out a group of eight kids sitting in a loose cluster under a tree. None of them faced each other or said a word. "That's your group over there." The kid shuffled off to join the loners, grabbing a spot beside them but not talking to anyone.

"I don't get the loners," Avery said, watching him go. "It's like, they want to be alone, but they like to hang out together."

"Yeah, they're freaks," Meredith agreed.

"Okay, next!"

A girl in a woven hemp shirt and long flowered skirt strolled up, and Meredith looked her up and down.

"Special interests?" Meredith asked.

"I'm really involved in recycling programs and trying to find renewable energy sources," the girl replied.

Meredith's boyfriend, Cameron, walked over just in time to hear this, and leaned over to whisper, "Eco-Maniac," in Meredith's ear.

"Good call, Cameron!" Meredith smiled proudly at her boyfriend. "Total tree-hugger!" She turned to the girl and handed her a diagram of the courtyard. "Now, if you go sit at this table," she began, marking the spot with a pink highlighter, "you'll find some people who are totally into the big paper versus plastic debate."

"Cool," the girl replied. "Peace." She wandered away, while Meredith smiled after her, a plastic smile plastered across her face.

Just then, Principal Dimly strode up to the table. "What is it, Daddy?" Meredith hissed, not looking at her father.

Principal Dimly held up the book he was thumbing through, *Running a Prison for Dummies*. "You were right, Pumpkin," he said. "It's all about order. It says so right here in chapter 32: 'Controlling the Population.' You're a prodigy. A genius. Which, of course, is in our genes. That's why they call it *genius*, you know."

"Daddy, I've told you fifty times that you may not speak to me during school hours," she snapped. "It doesn't look right." She shooed him away, adding, "I'm busy now, Daddy. Buh-bye!"

As her father slunk away, Meredith called, "Next!" A girl approached, wringing her hands nervously. She opened her mouth to introduce herself, but then she just burst into tears.

"Emo," Meredith declared, then explained to her friends, "That's short for emotional. Like, *over*-emotional!"

She made a mark on a copy of her diagram and handed it to the girl. In a super-sweet voice, she explained, "You're going to a really nice table where no one will bother you, okay? And I promise it will be the same table every day, because I know how upsetting change can be. Does that sound good?"

The girl nodded, sniffling, and made her way in the direction Meredith had indicated.

Cloe, Jade, Sasha and Yasmin strode past the table, too busy talking to notice the official check-in station.

"Oh no, they did *not* just walk past us without checking in," Quinn cried.

"Maybe they just didn't notice my twelve-foot, professionally printed banner," Meredith suggested through clenched teeth.

Cameron's eyes followed Cloe, and he asked, "Who's that?"

Meredith froze, glaring at the girl who

had caught her boyfriend's attention, but trying not to show how mad she was. "No one you need to even think about, Cameron."

"They look kinda cool." Quinn interjected, checking out the girls' cool outfits.

Avery tried to shush Quinn, while Meredith slowly turned to shoot her friend a cold, calculating look.

"In a totally trashy, beneath our contempt, maybe we can find a little spare time to crush 'em into the dirt kind of way," Avery interjected, covering for her friend.

Meredith smiled in satisfaction. "No, Avery. We don't crush. We focus on the positive. We'll just help them find their way. Or else …"

But the girls floated past, entering the school, where they were surrounded by flocks of students all moving methodically with their new cliques. In the front hall, the cheerleaders were practicing a routine, while off to the side, the band rehearsed.

The four best friends looked around at the bustle of activity in awe. "Whoa," they murmured.

"Is it just me, or does all this look a little creepily well-organized?" Yasmin asked as a group of preps in matching khakis and sweaters passed on one side, while a cluster of Goths in coordinating all-black outfits wandered by on the other.

Just then, the bell rang, interrupting her train of thought.

"Better run!" Sasha declared. "Have a good day, girls!"

"See you at lunch!" Cloe added. The girls all waved goodbye, staring at their schedules as they headed off in opposite directions.

Chapter 3

Jade burst into the science laboratory, looking out of place in her cute skirt and tee in the roomful of science guys. Jade pulled on a pair of goggles and surveyed the room for an open spot at one of the lab tables.

While she looked around, a boy in horn-rimmed glasses and a short-sleeved button-down shirt approached. "Excuse me, but are you in the right place?" he asked.

Jade picked a spot, put on a lab coat to protect her cute little outfit, and grabbed a couple of test tubes. "You tell me," she replied, then turned her attention to the chemicals in front of her. "A little magnesium, some sodium salts, a pinch of perchlorate and a touch of strontium nitrate, and voila—"

Her concoction bubbled, sending up tiny colored sparks in a miniature fireworks display. The science geeks, who had gathered around to watch her experiment, burst into applause.

Dexter, the one who had spoken earlier, gasped, "You have some serious science skills! Would you consider joining our science team?"

"I could be talked into it," Jade agreed with a grin. "But first we need to make over these lab coats!"

With a few nips and tucks, she turned the plain white lab coats into stylish, tailored jackets. "There—isn't that better?" she asked, admiring her work as the gaggle of science boys showed off their new lab coats.

*   *   *

Sasha stood in the gym in front of a group of snotty-looking varsity cheerleaders who were running through a dull routine that Sasha and the other cheerleading hopefuls were supposed to learn for their audition. Sasha rolled her eyes.

"Is there a problem?" demanded Bethany, the head cheerleader.

"It's just that I was doing that routine in daycare," Sasha replied. "Don't you think our teams deserve cheers that aren't older than they are?"

"You got something better?" Bethany snapped, annoyed.

"You *know* I do," Sasha told her.

"So bring it." Bethany put her hands on her hips and tried to stare Sasha down, but Sasha just smiled.

"Girl, I brought it, I nailed it, I lent it to my friend's kid sister, and I borrowed it back while you were still figurin' out the beat." She tossed a CD in the squad's boom box, and turned the music up. Then she busted out some spectacular dance moves that left the rest of the squad stunned.

*   *   *

Out on the soccer field, Cloe drove the ball toward the goal, expertly weaving past everyone who tried to get in her way. She was unstoppable.

The huge goalie narrowed her eyes at Cloe, watching her approach. Cloe just grinned back confidently, then leapt into the air, kicking the ball past the goalie with such power and perfect aim that it embedded itself in the net behind her. The rest of the team stared at it dangling there, stunned.

"Not bad for a rookie," the goalie told her.

"Not bad, period!" one of Cloe's teammates exclaimed, running up to her and slapping her on the back.

Cameron watched admiringly from the

bleachers. "Wow, she's good," he exclaimed.

Next to him, Meredith glared at Cloe and grabbed her boyfriend's hand possessively. "It was a lucky shot," she muttered.

* * *

Jade sat behind a sewing machine in her Home-Ec class, rapidly running a length of bright red material through it. Mrs. Funk, her teacher, walked over and stared at Jade's creation skeptically, her face pinched into a frown.

"It's very red," she said.

Jade zipped through the final seam, snipped the thread and pushed the pile of red fabric toward her teacher. "It's very *you*," she insisted.

Mrs. Funk held it up uncertainly, but the red dress Jade had made really did set off her complexion perfectly. Mrs. Funk admired her new look in the mirror, then flashed her student a smile.

*   *   *

Yasmin stood outside the school music room, watching through the open doorway as students auditioned for the choir. She took a step forward, then shook her head and stepped back again.

Mr. Whitman, the music teacher, spotted her lurking in the doorway and called, "Would you care to join us?"

Yasmin froze. "Oh-I-" She took a step toward him, then turned on her heel and bolted out of the room, slamming directly into a jock named Dylan. They ended up sprawled on the floor in a tangle of arms and legs.

"Geez, why don't you watch where you're going?" Yasmin asked, struggling to disentangle herself.

Dylan didn't reply, and Yasmin insisted, "Hello? Are you blind?"

Dylan scrambled to his feet, shooting her a cool look. "No. Actually, I'm deaf."

Yasmin stood up and stared at him in

confusion. "What?"

"I'm deaf," he repeated.

"You don't sound deaf," Yasmin told him.

"Yeah, well, you don't look ignorant," he retorted. "But I guess you can't judge a book by its cover, can you?" With that, he stalked off, leaving her staring after him in embarrassment.

Yasmin hurried over to the cafeteria, eager to meet her friends for lunch. It had been a rough day so far, but she knew everything would seem better once she had her best friends around her. She saw them waiting at the entrance to the cafeteria, and a smile spread across her face. They caught up on their days while they made their way through the lunch line, and then headed out to the courtyard to find a table.

"Um, where do they think they're going to sit?" Avery whispered to Meredith at their table in the center of the courtyard. All the cliques were organized into their assigned tables, and this foursome had never gotten their assignments.

"Give me the seating chart," Meredith demanded. She grabbed the chart from Avery and headed for the girls.

"Hi guys," she said cheerfully. "I'm Meredith, your Student Body President. I saw you looking kind of lost, so I thought I'd come over to help you out."

"Thanks," Yasmin replied, "but I think we're good."

"It's no problem at all," Meredith told her. "I have the seating chart right here." Smiling brightly, she held the chart out to the girls, but none of them made a move to take it.

"Nah, I think we'd rather sit together," Yasmin insisted.

"But you aren't in the same group," Meredith snapped. "There's really not a table for that."

"That's okay." Yasmin started to walk away, and her friends followed her. "We'll find space somewhere."

"But that's not how the lunch courtyard works!" Meredith shouted after her.

"Don't worry, we'll figure something out," Yasmin called over her shoulder.

Furious, Meredith stalked back to her table, where Avery had been watching this exchange admiringly. "What are you looking at?" Meredith demanded.

"They're just awesome—uh, I mean, *awful*," Avery corrected herself. "Like, check out their clothes. Yuck! Just totally *awful*. You know?"

"Totally," Quinn agreed. "So what are we going to do about them?"

"We don't need to do a thing," Meredith told her. "My system is flawless. Check it out."

As Cloe, Jade, Sasha and Yasmin searched for a table together, the cliques that surrounded them snapped into action.

"Hey Jade!" Dexter called from the math and science table. "Check out this radical theorem. You'll definitely dig it."

Jade hurried over to check out what he was talking about, waving goodbye to her friends as she slid into a seat beside Dexter. "Catch you girls after school?" she called over her shoulder.

"Sasha, we need your help picking out our new pom poms!" Bethany waved Sasha over to the cheerleaders' table.

"We need to go over the routines for our next performance," Sasha told her friends, hurrying over to Bethany's table.

"Cloe! You have to see this!" shouted Angie, the soccer team's goalie, holding up Cloe's new jersey with her lucky number 7 on the back. Cloe rushed over to the soccer table to check it out.

Yasmin found herself standing in the middle of the courtyard, completely alone. "We'll sit together tomorrow," she muttered as she found a spot on a bench off to the side and quietly ate her lunch.

"See?" Meredith asked her friends. "They're no problem at all."

*   *   *

That night, Yasmin instant messaged Jade. "I'm stuck babysitting!" she wrote. "Come over and hang with me?"

"I'd love to, but I have to get to Mathletes," Jade typed back. "Let's meet up next week."

At the same time, Cloe was text messaging Sasha. "I'm *so* in the mood to catch a movie. Are you in?"

"Can't—I'm booked solid!" Sasha replied. "Let's definitely do it next week."

The first week of school flew by, and the four best friends barely managed to see each other. But once the weekend arrived, Yasmin was sure all that would change.

On Saturday, she ran up to the front door of Sasha's mansion and knocked eagerly. Sasha threw open the door to reveal three other cheerleaders clustered behind her, all in their uniforms and ready to leave.

"Hey, Girl!" Sasha exclaimed. "Long time no see. What's up?"

"We're supposed to go shopping today," Yasmin began, but then she glanced at the group of cheerleaders and added, "but it looks like you're busy. It's cool."

"Oh my gosh, I totally flaked!" Sasha cried. "I'm so sorry. I have practice with the girls right now. Can we do it next week?"

"Absolutely," Yasmin agreed. "It's no problem at all."

"You're the best!" Sasha squealed, giving her friend a quick hug before turning back to her fellow cheerleaders. "Come on, girls, let's go. See you next week, Yas, for sure. I'll call you, okay?"

"Sure," Yasmin replied. She watched Sasha and her new friends dash past, piling into a senior cheerleader's car, and sighed. It seemed like high school was changing everything, and not in a good way.

Chapter 4

"And that's how we stopped being best friends," Yasmin told her grandma. They sat side by side on Yasmin's bed, and Bubbie put her arm around her granddaughter, trying to cheer her up. It was the first day of school again, but this time, instead of planning to take on the school as a team, each of the girls was caught up in her own separate world.

"It'll be okay, Yasmin," her grandma reassured her. "You'll see. You girls have been best friends for so long, and you will be again, I just know it."

"We've hardly spoken in two years," Yasmin explained. "I just don't see things suddenly getting better."

"Sweetheart, it's a whole new year," Bubbie insisted. "You never know what a new year will bring."

Yasmin smiled up at her grandma, wiping tears from her eyes. "I hope you're right, Bubbie."

"Your Bubbie is always right!" her grandmother exclaimed. "Now come on, you better get ready—you don't want to be late for the first day of school!"

Yasmin threw on a fluttery skirt, a sparkly top, and a pair of high heels from her grandma. After a quick glance in the mirror, she grabbed her brother Manny and rushed outside.

"Are you ready for your first day of high school?" she asked her brother as they hopped into her convertible.

"I was *born* ready," he told her, examining his hair in the visor mirror. Grinning, she put the car's top down, and soon his perfectly groomed locks were in total disarray. "Nooo!" he complained, but Yasmin just laughed. Maybe it would be a great first day after all.

"You can always take the bus, you know," Yasmin told her brother.

"Are you kiddin' me? I have a reputation to protect," Manny replied.

"Then maybe you should borrow a headscarf from Bubbie next time," Yasmin suggested, giggling.

"I'd be careful, Yas," Manny warned her. "You don't know who you're messing with."

"Okay, Kiddo, whatever you say," Yasmin replied, ruffling his hair. "I'll see you after school."

She hurried to the front steps of the school, but not to meet up with her old best friends. Instead, she watched while Cloe walked in with the soccer team, Sasha strolled through the front doors with the cheerleading squad, and Jade went in with the math and science crowd.

They all made their way into the gym for their morning assembly and sat in designated spots with each of their cliques. Meredith stood behind a podium at the front of the room with Principal Dimly at her side, surveying the perfectly organized gymnasium.

"Perfect," Principal Dimly sighed. "A place for everyone, and everyone in their place."

"As it should be!" Meredith agreed.

Principal Dimly leaned over the microphone and announced, "Good morning and welcome to another great year at Carry Nation High School. Now, without further ado, please let me introduce your reigning president, my daughter, Meredith Baxter Dimly."

Meredith stepped up to the microphone and cleared her throat. "Thank you, Principal Dimly. And good morning everyone! I'm so thrilled to be here as your

Student Body President once again. For those of you who voted for me, thank you so much! And for those who didn't, I hope you learned your lesson this time." With a fake smile, she added, "Just kidding! I'm totally kidding!"

Her audience laughed uncertainly—she clearly hadn't been kidding.

"Anyway, I'm not here to talk politics," she continued. "I'm here to talk about the talent show, which I'm heading up again, and the fact that in addition to the coveted Golden Hatchet, our wonderful arts committee is providing a spectacular grand prize this semester: A full scholarship to the college of your choice!" The students all began talking excitedly, and Meredith shouted over them, "Amazing, isn't it? I'll be holding auditions all month, so sign up now!"

While she explained the audition schedule, Yasmin, perched at the far end of a bleacher high up in the gym, was busily taking notes on her reporter's pad for the school newspaper. Looking around, she shook her head at the obvious segregation throughout the gym: The slackers, marching band members, choir kids, artists, hip-hoppers, bikers, and dancers were all in their own separate groups, none of them daring to speak to anyone outside of their clique. She was so wrapped up in the rant she was scribbling that she leapt up, startled, when the bell rang, and her notes scattered around her. She scrambled to gather them up, and then headed for the bathroom.

But as she burst into the girls' bathroom, she spotted Jade leaning over the sink and carefully applying lip gloss. The two former best friends hadn't been alone together in two years, and Yasmin felt so uncomfortable that she almost turned to go. But then she took a deep breath and strode up to the sink next to Jade's, whipping out her own lip gloss.

"Hey," Yasmin said tensely, breaking the silence.

"Um, hi," Jade replied, not looking over at Yasmin.

Yasmin looked around nervously, but then she noticed Jade's lip gloss. "'Peach Party,' right?" she asked. "Great color."

Jade turned to her, excitedly, forgetting for a moment that they weren't friends anymore. "Thanks! I totally love it!"

"It's gorgeous!" Yasmin agreed. "I just got it!" She held up her own tube, and the girls shared a smile. But their smiles slipped away as they remembered that they weren't friends anymore.

"So, yeah… great gloss," Jade muttered.

"I know, right?" Yasmin agreed awkwardly. "Shiny."

"Definitely," Jade replied. "Very… shiny."

"Okay! So, I guess I better get to class." Jade slid her lip gloss back into her purse and shot Yasmin a tentative smile.

"Yeah, me too," Yasmin said. "Well, have a good class."

"Thanks. You, too," Jade called over her shoulder.

"See ya," Yasmin shouted as the door slammed shut behind her former friend. With a sigh, she added quietly, "I miss you."

*   *   *

In the music room, Dylan sat behind the piano, hitting the same chord over and over. He stopped, cradling his head in his hands in frustration. Mr. Whitman, the music teacher, approached from the corner where he had been listening to this performance and put his hands on Dylan's shoulders comfortingly.

"Hey, Mr. Whitman," Dylan said, looking up at the teacher.

"That was great," Mr. Whitman told him. "You've been holding out on me."

"What do you mean?" Dylan asked.

"All this time, I thought you were just a cool jock," Mr. Whitman replied.

"Whatever." Dylan got up from the piano and started to leave, but the teacher put out a hand to stop him.

"Wait, Dylan. What's going on?" he inquired.

"Nothing," Dylan snapped. But then he met the teacher's eyes and saw the concerned expression there. "It's just that I miss it. I miss music," he admitted.

"I can understand that," Mr. Whitman agreed. "But you don't have to keep missing it, you know?"

"What are you *talking* about?" Dylan demanded. "I lost my hearing. And you can't play music if you can't hear it."

"But you *can* hear," Mr. Whitman insisted. "With these." He held up his hands and wiggled his fingers at Dylan, but Dylan just shook his head.

"Here, let me show you," Mr. Whitman continued. He took Dylan's hands and laid them on top of the piano, then played a few chords. "Feel that?"

"Sure," Dylan replied. "But that doesn't mean I can play it."

"True," his teacher admitted. "But what

about this?" He led Dylan over to a vintage record player, slid a vinyl album onto the player and turned it on. Mr. Whitman started scratching the album, DJ style, and placed Dylan's hand on the nearby speaker. "Feel that?" he asked.

"Yeah," Dylan agreed.

"Try it," Mr. Whitman suggested.

Dylan tried a few scratches, and grinned. "You're a natural!" Mr. Whitman exclaimed.

"Whitman, you're a weird dude ... but you're okay," Dylan told him

"Thanks." The teacher smiled back at him and added, "Wanna learn a few tricks?"

Chapter 5

That afternoon, Meredith and her two best friends sat behind a table draped with a banner reading "Audition for the Talent Show!" at the entrance to the lunch courtyard.

"So what are you going to do for the talent show this year?" Quinn asked her.

"It doesn't matter," Avery pointed out. "You know she'll win anyway."

Meredith smiled sweetly at her two friends. "Just because I'm going to win doesn't mean I don't owe all my fans an awesome show."

A kid in a court jester hat and parachute pants approached and started to juggle.

"Juggling?" Meredith sneered at the boy. "Please. That is *so* not talent show material."

"But wait," the juggler protested. "I can set the balls on fire." He whipped out a lighter and started juggling the fireballs, crying "Ow! Ow! Ow!" as each fell into his hands. But Meredith didn't notice—she had turned her attention to Cameron, who she had just seen strolling over to talk to Cloe.

"Oh no, he didn't!" she hissed. She scooped up her dog and looked her straight in the eye. "Paris, Mommy needs your help. Now, go over there and make sure Cameron doesn't talk to the evil soccer skank anymore, okay?" Paris wagged her tail and yipped eagerly. Meredith sat down and Paris scurried toward Cloe, her nails clicking against the tile floor as she hurried to complete her mission.

Cameron stood next to Cloe, trying to summon the courage to speak to her.

"Hi," he said finally.

"Me?" Cloe asked, shocked that he was talking to her.

"Yeah," he replied, not meeting her eyes.

"Oh." Cloe blushed, but she couldn't help smiling. "Wow." She was so mesmerized by Cameron that she didn't notice Paris tugging at her shoelaces to untie them. Then Paris grabbed Cloe's sock in her teeth, braced herself against the ground, and tugged hard. Cloe stumbled, and as she tried to regain her balance, she tripped over her untied shoelaces and her tray went flying, landing on Jade at the bottom of the stairs. "Cloe!" Jade cried as her lunch tray flew out of her hands. "Geez, you are such a klutz!"

Jade stumbled into a trashcan and rolled towards Sasha's table, food from her tray splattering everywhere. A mass of purple Jell-O landed on Sasha's uniform, and she leapt up, horrified. "Oh no, you didn't!" Sasha squealed. She whirled to see Jade sprawled nearby and shouted, "Jade! You totally did that on purpose!"

She leapt out of her seat and slipped on a skateboard that someone had left nearby and plowed straight into Yasmin, knocking her down.

Her hair in disarray and her shirt dripping with food from her lunch tray, Yasmin picked herself up and cried, "You ruined my hair, you stupid … *cheerleader*."

Sasha scooped a handful of Jell-O off of her uniform and tossed it at Yasmin. "You did *not* just say that," she hissed. "Keep talking, Yasmin—maybe someday you'll say something intelligent."

Yasmin wiped some spaghetti off of her shirt and threw it at Sasha in retaliation. "Oh, Sasha, you're not as mean as people say you are." As the glob of spaghetti smacked into her former friend, she added, "You're worse!"

Soon all four girls were yelling and throwing the remains of their lunches at each other. Paris leapt out of the way and knocked over the bust of Principal Dimly that stood at the center of the courtyard in her rush to get back to Meredith. Cloe, Jade, Sasha and Yasmin noticed the falling statue at the same moment and they all dove to catch it, but it shattered on the terra cotta tiles that lined the courtyard. They all laid facedown, panting, as Principal Dimly approached.

"Now you've done it," Principal Dimly shouted. "You crossed the line, and someone's going to pay. If you don't tell me exactly what happened, and I mean now, you're all headed straight for detention."

The girls just stared at him, and that afternoon, they all found themselves sitting as far apart as possible at the single big table in the center of the library, which served as the detention room after school. They refused to look at each other, and brushed angrily at their food-spattered outfits.

"I can't believe Dimly wouldn't even let me change first," Jade complained. "I have a spare outfit in my locker."

"I don't even *belong* here," Yasmin muttered, furious.

"Neither do I," Sasha hissed.

"Oh, quit whining," Cloe interrupted. The other three turned to glare at her. "What?" she demanded. "Complaining won't help, *and* it's annoying."

"Hey, you started it with your famous klutz act," Jade retorted.

"Come on, I tripped!" Cloe protested. "I'm sure nothing like that's ever happened to you, Little Miss Perfect."

"That is *so* like you," Jade declared. "You can never admit your mistakes."

"How would you know what any of us are like?" Sasha demanded. "We haven't spoken since you dumped us to become queen of the dorks!"

"Me?" Jade cried. "You haven't said a word to any of us since you went all cheerleader." In a high-pitched, mocking voice, she added, "'I'm not a snob. I'm just better than you are.'"

"I didn't stop talking to you!" Sasha shouted. "You stopped talking to *me!*"

"Whatever, Sasha," Cloe replied. "We know we aren't good enough for you anymore. But at least we don't have to buy our friends with our daddies' bank accounts."

"That's because you don't have a dad or a bank account," Sasha snapped. Jade and Yasmin stared at her, stunned, while Cloe tried to hold back her tears.

"Stop it!" Yasmin exclaimed. "Just stop it."

Sasha stared at her hands, ashamed of what she had said. "Cloe, I'm so sorry. I can't believe I said that."

"It's okay," Cloe replied softly.

"No, it's not," Sasha insisted. "You were totally there for me when my parents split. I'll never forget that. At least, not again."

"We used to do everything together," Yasmin interjected. "What happened to us?"

"I can't even remember," Cloe told her. "We just all started doing different stuff."

"And only hanging out with people who do the same things we do," Jade added.

"It's the cliques," Yasmin explained.

"Please, I am *not* in a clique," Sasha protested. "I hang out with a lot of different cheerleaders…" Noticing the girls' raised eyebrows, she sighed. "Oh. Okay, yeah, I only hang out with cheerleaders. Guilty as charged."

"Hey, we're all in cliques," Yasmin declared. "That's just how high school works. "You're a cheerleader, Cloe's a jock, and Jade's in with the over-achieving school nerds."

"They aren't nerds," Jade interrupted. "They're really interesting people."

"I'm sure they are, but there's no way I'll ever get to see that because they're not in my clique," Yasmin replied.

"So what do we do?" Cloe asked. "I miss you guys so much."

"I really miss you girls, too," Sasha agreed. "I guess I didn't realize how much until now."

"Well then, it's time to take control of our lives, and our friendships," Yasmin announced. "We only have ourselves to blame for losing each other, but now we can choose to be friends with each other *and* with our cliques."

Yasmin put her hand in the middle of the table. "Best friends forever?"

Cloe, Jade, and Sasha covered her hand with theirs and shouted, "Best friends forever!"

*   *   *

"I can't *believe* them!" Meredith shouted in the security booth where she and her friends were spying on the girls using the school's closed-circuit cameras. "They are not above the rules! If they think they can just ignore a system that works perfectly, they'd better just watch their backs!" She whirled to face Cameron and added, "This is all your fault! If you hadn't walked up to that soccer joke, I wouldn't have had to take action, and those bimbettes wouldn't be together again, plotting against my system!"

Turning to Avery, she added, "Mark down one demerit for Cameron."

"What?!" Cameron cried.

"I'm sorry, did you say something?" Meredith asked coolly.

Cameron stared at her, but seeing the fury in her eyes, he dropped his gaze. "No ... ma'am."

"I didn't think so," Meredith snapped. "Well, if all else fails, I always have my secret weapon!"

She whipped out her Swarovski crystal-encrusted jump drive, and Avery and Quinn gasped.

"I really don't think this calls for the jump

drive, Meredith," Avery said nervously.

"What are you going to use that for?" Quinn asked.

"I don't know yet," Meredith replied, "but I'm sure I'll think of something good."

Chapter 6

That night, Yasmin couldn't have been happier. She had just applied a cucumber facial mask and was dancing around her room, singing "La Cucaracha" at the top of her lungs. Overhearing her, Yasmin's grandma hurried into the room and started singing and dancing along. Manny walked by and burst into laughter at the wacky performance in Yasmin's room. He whipped out his cell phone to capture it on video, and Yasmin and Bubbie waved playfully at him.

"I *know* this'll come in handy for

something," Manny muttered.

Yasmin and her grandma finished their song and collapsed on Yasmin's bed.

"So tell me, Honey, why so happy?" Bubbie asked. "Did you meet a boy?"

Yasmin shook her head. "No boy, Bubbie. It's Sasha, Cloe, and Jade. We're a team again! And we're going to be friends with everyone, not just stick to our own little cliques."

"That sounds good to me," Bubbie told her. "I mean, if I didn't get to know people outside my own group, do you think you'd be living with fifteen Latin Jews?"

"I guess not," Yasmin agreed.

"You girls are doing the right thing," Bubbie insisted. "You walk into that school and socialize with whoever you like. Walk in with your head held high, and walk in with these gorgeous new shoes!"

She pulled a pair of heels out of a shopping bag at her feet, and Yasmin squealed, "Te amo, Bubbie!"

* * *

"I love the smell of retail in the morning," Sasha sighed, surveying the stores spread out around her best friends and her at their favorite mall, the Grove. Cloe, Jade, Sasha and Yasmin were shopping together for the first time in two years, and they were loving it!

"That's my Sasha!" Yasmin exclaimed. "I've missed you guys so much! I can't believe it's been two whole years—that's like, *forever*! So what's the latest and greatest?"

The girls headed into their first store as Jade answered, "Still hiding everything from my parents."

"That must suck," Yasmin replied, but Jade just shrugged.

"It's not that bad. It just means I spend a lot of time changing clothes in sketchy bathrooms," she explained.

"It's so weird," Yasmin told her. "Fashion is like your superpower. You shouldn't have to hide it."

The most fabulous, fierce, fantastic foursome on their first day of high school - best friends forever!

"I'm going to own the Science Club," Jade said.

Sasha totally owns cheerleading.

Bend it like Cloe!

"Hi," says Jade uncomfortably to Yasmin, who used to be her BFF. "Well, I have to get to class, so see you around."

It seemed like high school was changing everything, and not in a good way.

"We used to do everything together,"
Yasmin interjected. "What's happened to us?"

"Well, it's time to take control of our lives and our friendships,"
Yasmin announced. "Best friends forever?"

"We do what we planned to do, we stay friends,
we hang out together, it's not like anyone can stop us."

"Now that's what I call ... Clown Couture," said Jade to the other girls.

As Jade finishes attaching the letters that spell out 'Brats' on a jacket, she looks at the letters, shrugs and replaces the 's' with 'z' – much hipper! The Bratz are born!

The fab foursome begin to rehearse for the talent show, and officially name themselves 'Bratz'.

"Meredith, this one's for you!" The Bratz started
singing and they sounded totally amazing.

"Oh my gosh, a red carpet performance!" Sasha exclaimed.

The Bratz look totally dazzlin'! Dunked in glitter from head to toe, they perform 'Open Eyes' on the red carpet.

BFF's!!

"Please," Jade protested. "That's, like, the textbook definition of a superpower. It's the thing in your life that you're really amazing at, but that you have to hide from the world so people think you're normal."

"I guess," Yasmin agreed. Turning to Cloe, she asked, "How 'bout you, Clo,? What have you been up to?"

"Nothing but soccer and school," Cloe admitted. "I'm so ready to have fun, and I've been trying to save up for a camcorder. I was really hoping to make my first movie this year. But I have to focus on soccer so I can get a scholarship."

"How's your mom doing?" Yasmin asked.

"All she does is work," Cloe said.

"That's tough," Jade replied, as she guided her friends toward a cool new store.

"Tell me about it," Cloe agreed. "How 'bout your parents, Sash?"

"Still not speaking to each other," Sasha told her friends. "I just wish they could figure out a way to get along."

"I hear you." Cloe turned to Yasmin. "And what about you, Yas?"

"Nothing much," Yasmin said with a shrug. "Still sharing a bathroom with fifteen relatives—the usual."

"Come on, I know that's not the whole story," Sasha insisted. "Spill!"

Yasmin stopped in the middle of the store and looked at each of her friends in turn. She drew in a deep, shaky breath and admitted, "Well, I started writing some songs, and I think they actually sound pretty good. But mostly I've just been missing you guys."

"Speaking of guys," Jade interrupted, "Check him out!"

Dylan strolled by and barely glanced at Yasmin.

"Girl, he totally just checked you out!" Sasha squealed.

"Are you kidding?" Yasmin asked. "Dylan hates me. Anyway, he's really not my type."

"You have a type?" Jade teased.

"Ha-ha," Yasmin replied. "Look, Dylan never looks me in the eyes, he can never remember my name, and he's certainly never asked me out." Her friends shot her a meaningful look, and she gasped, "Oh my gosh! He's crazy about me!"

Smiling at her friends, she added, "And I never would have figured it out without you girls. I love you all so much." She pulled them into a group hug and said, "Swear we won't ever let anything break us up again?"

Sasha nodded and held out her pinkie. "Pinkie swear."

"Pinkie swear!" her friends exclaimed in unison, hooking their pinkie fingers together.

*　　*　　*

"I think we're making this way too complicated," Jade told her friends as they strode into school together the next morning. "I mean, if we want to be friends, we just have to be friends."

"I totally agree," Yasmin chimed in. "We'll just lead by example."

They headed for the quad, where the girl jocks immediately spotted Cloe and waved her over. She smiled and waved back, but kept walking. Jade did the same with the science nerds, and Sasha with the cheerleaders. They grabbed a table together in the center of the quad.

"Are people staring?" Cloe asked nervously.

"Oh yeah," Sasha told her, scoping out the furtive glances every clique was casting in their direction, plus the outright glares from Meredith's table.

"Awkward," Jade whispered.

"Super weird," Sasha agreed.

"I think it's time for Plan B," Yasmin declared.

"Yay!" Cloe cheered. "Plan B!" She paused, then asked, "Um, what's Plan B?"

"Operation Mingle!" Yasmin announced.

The girls hit the hallways and fanned out

to start talking to different cliques.

Sasha ran into a geek in the girls' bathroom and gave her a quick makeover. The girl gave her a huge smile, her braces and her new lip gloss glinting under the florescent lights.

Cloe found a group of mimes practicing in a nearby classroom, and silently helped them mime some soccer kicks and passes. The mimes mimicked her movements perfectly, and she announced, "Now you're ready to try it with a real ball!" The mimes stared at her, horrified that she had broken the silence, but they followed her out to the field and even managed to score a few points against Cloe and her soccer buddies.

After the game, Cloe introduced Yasmin to one of the girl jocks, and Yasmin introduced the girl to the collection of high heels in her locker. She grabbed a pair and convinced the girl to try them on, but when the jock tried to take a step in them, she almost tumbled over. Yasmin rushed over to steady her, and the girl complained, "Don't you have a fancy pair of sneakers in the Yasmin collection? Anything under, say, six inches? This is shoeicide!"

"Come on, my *sole* sister," Yasmin insisted. "By the time we're through, you'll be sauntering down the hall like a supermodel."

"But I just want to make sure I stay vertical," the girl protested.

"Stay vertical?" Yasmin cried. "Honey, when I'm finished with you, you'll be playing your next soccer game in stilettos!"

In the math classroom, Jade drew a football formation on the chalkboard for a roomful of jocks. "What's a touchdown, plus an extra point, plus a safety, divided by a field goal?" She wrote the equation as she spoke.

"Uh … three?" a football jock suggested.

Jade threw her arms over her head in triumph. "It's good!" she exclaimed, as all the jocks cheered and gave each other high fives.

In the music room, Yasmin approached Dylan, trying to practice the sign for "I'd like to be your friend" as she walked. She repeated it to herself as she headed toward him, but Dylan stopped her.

"Um, I know we jocks have a reputation for being dumb, but I can speak and read lips perfectly," Dylan told her. "So, do you really want me to clean my room?" he asked, repeating Yasmin's hand movements.

"What?" Yasmin cried. "Oh, no! I just wanted to see if maybe we could, maybe talk sometime or something. Or if you're busy right now, you could call me . . . although how would you call me? I mean, since you're … ugh! I am *so lame*! Sorry to have bothered you. I'm leaving now."

She was too embarrassed to notice Dylan smiling after her as she scurried out of the room.

After school, Cloe was kicking some balls into the soccer goal while Cameron practiced at the other end of the field. He paused to watch Cloe make a few goals, then ran over to join her. "Killer shots!" he exclaimed.

"Oh, thanks," she replied. She pushed her hair out of her face and smiled at him.

"I was watching your technique, and I think I have a few ideas to help you make it even better," Cameron told her.

"I'm listening," Cloe said.

He stepped behind her and put his hands on her waist. "Your power comes from your core," he explained, twisting her waist so her right hip was cocked back. "Use your hip to give you more strength and follow through with a quick, composed motion. Try it."

Cameron set a soccer ball in front of her foot, then stood in front of the goal, waiting.

"Okay, hip back," Cloe began, pivoting as

Cameron had just shown her. She lined up her kick and slammed her foot into the ball, knocking it straight into Cameron, who stumbled back into the goal.

"Oh my gosh!" Cloe ran toward Cameron and helped him up. "Geez, I'm such a klutz. I'm so sorry! Are you okay?"

"I'm good," Cameron panted. "And Cloe? That was a great shot."

Neither of them saw Meredith glaring at them from the bleachers, or stalking away, enraged, as they smiled shyly at each other.

*　　*　　*

Meredith rushed back to her place and called Quinn and Avery, who hurried over to find their friend already lounging on a float in her pool. Paris bobbed beside her on her own pool float, wearing her own tiny sunglasses and bikini.

Meredith's little sister, Cherish, spread out her yoga mat beside the pool, settled into the lotus position, closed her eyes, and started chanting, "Ohmmmm."

"Oh my gosh, Cherish, *what* are you doing?" Meredith demanded, sitting up so fast on her pool float that she almost tipped it over.

"Trying to imagine you with a personality," Cherish replied.

"Can't you find somewhere *else* to be a freak?" Meredith asked. "Ugh. You are *so* embarrassing."

"I'm busy right now," Cherish declared. "Can I ignore you some other time?"

"Did you forget, Munchkin? *Everyone* does what I say," Meredith informed her sister.

"Not from what I saw at school today," Cherish pointed out.

Avery and Quinn, emerging from the house in their swimsuits, overheard this last exchange. "Ouch," Avery murmured.

"Whatever," Meredith snapped. "This is just a temporary loss of control. I can assure you, I *will* bring order back to our school. I just need a plan."

She pulled off her sunglasses and gnawed on the end thoughtfully while her friends lowered themselves into the pool. "I've got it!" Meredith announced suddenly.

"Okay, when was I at the height of my popularity?" Meredith asked as her friends swam toward her.

"Last year's talent show?" Avery suggested.

"Ooh, wait, I know this one!" Quinn cried.

"Yes, Quinn?" Meredith inquired.

"Your Super Sweet Sixteen party," Quinn announced.

"She's right," Avery replied. "That was, like, the most amazing party ever. Everyone was sucking up to you for weeks beforehand just to get an invitation."

"I love it when people suck up to me," Meredith sighed, gazing up at the sky as she remembered all the favors she'd been able to command when people were desperate to get an invite to her party. Then she turned to her friends and declared, "So it's settled. I'm throwing another Super Sweet Sixteen."

"But you already turned sixteen," Quinn protested.

"I'm throwing. Another. Super Sweet Sixteen," Meredith insisted. "And I'll get MTV to film the whole event. The producer is my mom's best friend, so that's no problem. I'm sure she can get DJ Wax to host it, too—he's my absolute fave!" She relaxed back onto her pool float, relieved that she had solved the problem. "I feel *so* much better. Don't you?"

"Why is she throwing another Sweet Sixteen?" Quinn whispered to Avery.

"I'm not sure exactly," Avery replied.

"I'll use the invitations to bully everyone into going back to their cliques," Meredith continued.

"No cliquey—no ticky!" Quinn chimed in. Her friends shared an evil smile just as a shadow fell across Cherish.

She opened her eyes to see Manny standing over her. "Hey, Cherish. Missed you at ballet," he said.

"You do ballet?" Quinn cried, giggling.

"Hey, it's a great place to meet chicks," Manny explained. "Like this lovely lady here." He ran his hand through his hair and gave Cherish his most dazzling smile, but she turned her back on him and tried to resume her meditation.

"Hey, isn't that Yasmin's little brother?" Avery asked her friends.

"Yeah," Quinn told her. "What's he doing here?"

Manny noticed the girls looking at him and gave them a nod. "Lookin' good, Mamacitas."

"Gross," Avery whispered, but Meredith paddled her pool float over toward Manny, batting her eyelashes at him and giving him her most charming smile.

"Wow, you have the most incredible hair

ever," she exclaimed in her super-sweet voice.

"I know, right?" Manny agreed, flipping his hair back from his face.

"Totally," Meredith replied. "Come over here and tell me all your hair-care secrets." She patted a spot beside her on the pool float.

Manny paused for a moment, then handed his cell phone to Cherish. "Here, keep this dry," he told her. Then he jumped in the pool, fully clothed, and swam toward Meredith, his head held high to keep the water from ruining his hair.

"Your sister Yasmin is so sweet," Meredith announced as Manny treaded water alongside her. "What's it like to have such a perfect sister?"

"Yeah, what *is* that like?" Cherish interrupted.

"Perfect?" Manny cried. "Have you ever actually met her?"

"You're so funny," Meredith told him,

giggling. "I mean, she's just so good at *everything.*"

"You think so?" Manny asked. "Cherish, bring me my phone." Annoyed, Cherish walked over and dropped the phone in his hand. "Okay, check this out." He played the video of Yasmin and Bubbie singing, and Meredith smiled.

"She is so adorable!" Meredith gushed. "I have to add this to my special collection. Can you transfer it to this?" She pulled her crystal-studded jump drive off of Paris' collar, where she'd put it for safekeeping.

Manny happily plugged the jump drive into his phone and downloaded the video, certain he was on his way to being Meredith's next boyfriend and one of the rulers of the school.

Chapter 7

When Cloe, Jade, Sasha and Yasmin arrived at school the next morning, they were greeted by Meredith, Avery, and Quinn handing out flyers at the front door.

"It's Meredith's MTV My Super Sweet Sixteen," Quinn announced.

"It's gonna be even more incredibly fantastic than the last one," Avery added.

"It'll be hosted by DJ Wax himself!" Meredith declared. Everyone eagerly grabbed for the flyers, while Cloe, Jade, Sasha and Yasmin hung back, trying to figure out what was going on.

"She already had a Sweet Sixteen," Jade pointed out.

"So what do you think she's up to?" Cloe asked.

"Does it matter?" Sasha demanded. "It's a totally fabulous party!" With that, she led her friends over to Meredith and grabbed flyers for each of them.

After school that day, the girls headed back to the mall. They were all trying out new looks at the makeup counter when Sasha noticed Cloe hanging back, looking bummed out.

"Hey, Girlfriend," Sasha cried, "Why so serious? I mean, we're at the mall, *shopping*. How can you not be having fun?"

"I'm fine," Cloe told her, but Sasha shook her head.

"Riiight," Sasha replied. "Come on, I know you better than that."

"I can't go to Meredith's party," Cloe admitted. "I can't afford to buy anything new, and I'll just embarrass myself and all of you if I go."

"Come on, Cloe," Sasha insisted. "We've been pulled apart for too long, and it's *not* happening again. Especially not for Meredith's super-lame party."

"But Sasha, you guys have to go," Cloe replied. "And I have nothing to wear."

"Yes, you do," Sasha announced. She pulled two mall gift certificates out of her purse and held them out to Cloe. "I have two *guilt* certificates, one from my mom and one from my dad. Which means I have a spare!" Cloe shook her head, trying to refuse the gift certificate, but Sasha wouldn't hear of it. "Hey, having divorced parents has to have some benefits! And if it means I can help out a friend in need, then it can't be all bad."

"Now come on," Jade added. "We've got some serious shopping to do!"

*   *   *

"Good morning, Everyone," Meredith shouted into a glitzy pink megaphone at school the next morning. Along with Avery, Quinn, and Cameron, she was passing out brightly colored balloons to each student as they entered the school. "Pop your balloons to see where you'll be seated at Meredith's Super Sweet Sixteen party! Seating will be organized by groups. So if you don't belong to a group…I guess you can't come to my party."

Cloe, Jade, Sasha and Yasmin approached and shared a knowing look. "Hi, ladies!" Meredith greeted them. "These are for you." She handed each girl a balloon and added, "Go ahead—pop 'em!"

Each girl popped her balloon and removed an invitation with a prominent table assignment. And just as they'd feared, they were all seated at separate tables.

At lunch that day, everyone had re-arranged themselves according to Meredith's party seating chart, the cross-group conversations that the girls had started earlier that week brought to a screeching halt. "Well, she's brought back the cliques," Jade sighed.

"So what do we do now?" Cloe asked.

"We do what we planned to do," Yasmin announced. "We stay friends. We hang out together. It's not like anyone can stop us."

A flock of cheerleaders flounced over, pom poms in hand. Bethany stepped forward and pulled Sasha aside. "So, we've been talking. And, um, you're a really great cheerleader, and we really want you to be part of our team. But if you don't want to hang out with us, then maybe you just don't have the right kind of school spirit for the job."

"So if I'm not part of your clique, I'm off the squad?" Sasha demanded.

"Pretty much," Bethany agreed. "Think it over." With that, she and the other cheerleaders flounced away.

A group of science boys hurried over and surrounded Jade. "You either need to spend more time practicing for the Science

Olympics with us, or we need to drop you from the roster," Dexter explained.

"Dexter, don't be like that," Jade protested, but he just shook his head.

"I'm afraid it's not up to me," he told her. "That's just the way things work here at Carry Nation." With that, they headed off, leaving the four best friends alone again.

"Well, I guess we can always talk on the phone and hang out on the weekends, right?" Cloe said.

"I just can't believe how evil Meredith is," Sasha sighed.

"So let's not go to her party," Yasmin suggested. "She's trying to force us apart, but I say if we can't go to her party on our own terms, then it's not worth going at all."

"But Yas, it's gonna be an amazing party!" Sasha protested.

"And if we don't go, we'll probably be branded as total losers and outcasts," Jade added. But then she met Yasmin's determined gaze and nodded resolutely. "But

I'm willing to take that risk. I'm with Yasmin."

"Me too!" Cloe chimed in.

"But ..." Sasha complained.

"Sasha!" Jade cried.

"Okay, okay," Sasha agreed. "It's just that I had this gorgeous new outfit all picked out ... but friends are more important than fashion, right?"

"Right!" her friends declared.

*   *   *

Cloe returned from soccer practice the next day to find beautifully prepared platters spread over every available surface. "Wow, Mom, this looks amazing!" she called, looking around for Katie. "This must be for a major party."

When Katie didn't answer, Cloe wandered into her mom's room and found her sprawled across the bed.

"Mom? What's wrong?" Cloe asked. "Are you sick?"

"I just need a little sleep," Katie murmured.

Cloe laid her hand on Katie's forehead, looking at her mom with concern. "You're burning up," Cloe declared. "You can't work like this."

"Are you kidding?" Katie cried. "I have to do this party! I already bought everything, and anyway, they're counting on me! Just wake me up in a couple of hours, okay honey?"

"Okay," Cloe agreed. "Just get some rest." Katie closed her eyes and immediately fell back asleep. Cloe tiptoed out of the room, quietly closing the door behind her.

She walked into her own bedroom and speed-dialed her three best friends, getting them all on a conference call.

"What's up, Cloe?" Yasmin asked.

"It's an emergency," Cloe declared. "I need your help."

Within minutes, all four girls stood in Cloe's kitchen, staring at the platters spread out in front of them.

"So we need to make a hundred and fifty

of each dish," Cloe explained.

"Um, you want me to cook?" Sasha asked. "Girl, I burn *water*!"

"Come on, we can do it," Yasmin insisted. "Cloe, your catering cavalry has arrived. Lead the way!"

Cloe whipped out the recipes and started dividing up tasks among her friends. Soon they were all stirring, mixing, rolling and baking. When the flour settled, the platters and trays were all brimming with delicious-looking food, and the girls were covered in batter, but totally proud of themselves.

"We did it!" Cloe exclaimed, slumping into a chair at the kitchen table. Her friends sat down beside her, exhausted but happy.

"I knew we could!" Yasmin declared.

"Me, too!" Sasha agreed. Her friends raised her eyebrows at her. "What? I did!"

"We totally rocked this kitchen," Jade chimed in.

Just then, Katie dashed into the kitchen,

looking frantic. "Cloe, you didn't wake me up! It's five o'clock, and I have so much to do!"

"All done," Cloe told her, indicting the piles of food in the kitchen.

"Oh my gosh," Katie murmured. "Who did this?"

"We did!" Sasha exclaimed.

"Amazing," Katie cried, fighting back tears of joy. "You girls are absolute angels."

"We are, aren't we?" Cloe joked.

"It was a breeze!" Sasha added. Her friends stared at her, and she shrugged. "What? It was!"

Katie was listening to a message on her cell phone, and looking more and more upset with each passing moment.

"Mom, what is it?" Cloe asked.

"My servers have the same cold I came down with," Katie explained. "They aren't coming tonight. The biggest party of my career starts in two hours, and I don't have a single server."

The four best friends exchanged looks,

then all exclaimed, "We'll do it!"

"That's sweet girls, but before you say yes, I think you should know that it's Meredith's Sweet Sixteen," Katie told them.

"*Mom!* Are you kidding?" Cloe wailed.

"It was too much money to turn down," Katie replied. "But I'm just going to cancel."

The girls stared at the floor, but then Yasmin jumped in. "I think this is perfect. This way, we can be together at Meredith's party, *and* help out Cloe's mom."

"Sounds good to me," Sasha agreed.

"I can see us now," Jade added. "Fabulous tops, smokin' skirts, and killer boots. We are gonna own that party!"

"Um, yeah, there's just one little thing," Katie interrupted. "It's a circus-themed party, so Meredith bought some outfits she wanted the servers to wear."

The girls arrived at Meredith's party that night decked out in clown costumes, complete with poofy satin pants, frizzy clown wigs, red noses, and giant shoes. The girls hung their heads, totally humiliated, as Meredith circled them, inspecting her servers, before finally declaring, "Perfect!"

As Meredith strutted off, Katie said, "If you guys want to back out, I totally understand."

"No way!" Jade replied. "I just need five minutes with my Fashion Emergency Kit, and we'll be good to go!" She held up a cute houndstooth tote and pulled the girls into the kitchen.

"Ooh, and I've got my Makeup Essentials Kit," Sasha added, pulling out a black bag.

"Awesome!" Jade cried. "Let the magic begin!"

She tossed aside the wigs, noses, and shoes, then snipped and sewed rapidly, turning the costumes into flared shirts topped with form-fitting tanks, while Sasha gave each of the girls a makeover and added cute accessories from her bag. The girls put on their new outfits and ran into the bathroom to check themselves out.

"We look incredible!" Cloe murmured.

"Now that's what I call Clown Couture!" Jade declared. She handed each of her friends a pair of ballet flats she'd fashioned out of the leftover material, and the girls slipped them on, completing their look.

They stepped outside carrying their appetizer trays just in time to see Meredith parading out on a giant circus elephant, a pink plume sticking up from its head. Wearing a diamond-studded tiara, Meredith waved like a beauty queen in a parade. Around her, jugglers and fire eaters and acrobats performed while MTV cameras captured the action.

"Hi everyone!" Meredith exclaimed. "Hi MTV! It's me, Meredith, and this is my Super Sweet Sixteen party! Isn't it amazing?"

Heads turned, but not to look at her. Everyone was staring at Cloe, Jade, Sasha and Yasmin, looking totally hot in their Jadeified costumes. "Candied quiche and pineapple puffs, anyone?" Sasha called, and the crowd mobbed her and her friends.

"Hello, People!" Meredith shouted. "I'm up here!" Avery, Quinn and Cameron cheered her on, but everyone else at the party had flocked over to her four waitresses. Meredith climbed down off the elephant and stalked over to the girls with her friends following her. She pushed her way through the crowd to reveal the girls, their trays now empty. "Well, don't you guys look adorable," she hissed. "But you aren't here to look adorable. You're here to *work*." Turning to Cloe, she asked, "It's Clover, right?"

"Cloe," Cloe told her.

"Whoops!" Meredith replied dismissively. "Well, we are all dying of thirst here, so could you be a doll and get us some sodas. I'll take mine with a slice of lime." She started to leave, then turned back and added, "No, make that a lemon." She turned on her heel, then paused and said, "With a cherry. Take the stem off and put in two umbrellas, one green, one yellow. 'Kay?"

"Listen, Miss Thing—" Sasha began, but

Jade put her hand over Sasha's mouth to stop her.

"Make sure your friends keep a cork in it," Meredith ordered Cloe. "I wouldn't want to have to fire your mother. Again."

Cameron shot Cloe an apologetic glance, but followed Meredith when she stalked away.

"What was she talking about?" Yasmin asked Cloe.

"Nothing," Cloe told her. "Come on, we've got work to do."

While the girls circulated with their trays, Meredith hopped onto a stage she'd had built in her backyard. Next to her, DJ Wax spun some hip tracks, but Meredith interrupted to have him announce the official start of her party.

"Welcome to the outrageousness of outrageousness, the coolest of cool, the fabulous Meredith's MTV My Super Sweet Sixteen Party," he read from a card she handed him, sounding bored. "I'm DJ Wax, and I'll be spinning tunes that are beyond cool. And your hostess asked me to remind you that if you don't sit at your assigned tables, you'll be kicked out."

Meredith grabbed the microphone from him and exclaimed, "Just kidding! Anyway, there's plenty of yummy food and drinks, so just look for a clown with a tray! They're here to serve you, so work 'em hard! Now, let's party!"

DJ Wax pumped up the music and everyone hit the dance floor, grooving with their separate cliques. Cloe, Jade, Sasha and Yasmin wove through the crowd, busily distributing food.

Meredith leapt onstage again and exclaimed, "For the first super-fun event of my super-cool evening, it's time for *the* entertainment of the night—me!"

Dramatic laser lighting flooded the yard, and a huge spotlight hit Meredith in a sequined costume, surrounded by four male dancers in leotards. "And now I'll be singing my latest tune, which I like to call 'Fabulous!'" she announced. She launched into the song, and when it was over, she struck a pose while the audience applauded politely.

"Thank you *so* much," she cried. "Now, for a special treat, I want to invite my dear, dear friend to go next."

At the popular girls' table, Avery and Quinn both rushed to apply fresh lip gloss, primping in their compact mirrors. "I can't believe she's letting me go first!" Avery exclaimed.

"What are you talking about?" Quinn replied. "She talking about *me*."

She started to get up, but then Meredith continued, "Yazzie, darling. A little birdie told me that you just love to sing."

A group of perky circus performers ushered Yasmin up to the stage, despite her attempts to escape.

"This is going to be fantastic!" Meredith squealed. She handed Yasmin the microphone, then trotted off stage, leaving Yasmin alone to face the crowd.

"Come on, Yasmin," Meredith called. "Show us what you can do!"

Yasmin spotted her friends in the crowd and smiled weakly. "We love you, Yasmin!" they cheered. But Yasmin shook her head and handed the microphone back to Meredith.

"Oh, dear," Meredith cooed. "She is so adorably shy, isn't she? Well, I have had the privilege of seeing her perform, and I want to share it with all of you. You are in for a treat!" The lights strung over the backyard dimmed, and a huge projection screen was lowered behind the stage. On it appeared the video of Yasmin and Bubbie singing "La Cucaracha."

Yasmin covered her face with her hands as the crowd burst into hysterical laughter. As she ran off the stage in tears, Dylan grabbed some friends and started a conga line, imitating Yasmin and Bubbie's dance from the video. Yasmin's friends caught on and joined him, and DJ Wax threw on a tune to keep the conga line going. Soon the whole crowd was part of it, and everyone had forgotten about the embarrassing video that had started it all.

Everyone, that is, except Meredith. She ran onstage and yelled at DJ Wax, "Do something about this!"

"I'm on it," he replied, and cranked up the volume.

"That's not what I meant!" Meredith shouted. She pulled the plug on the sound system, and the crowd groaned. Taking the mic, she asked, "Would you like me to sing something else for you?" But no one was paying any attention to her, and she slunk off the stage, defeated.

Yasmin started circulating with another hors d'oeuvre tray, still trying to avoid everyone's eyes. As she rounded a corner, she nearly bumped into Dylan, and jerked back to stop herself. "Oh, I'm sorry!" she cried. "Um, foie gras mousse?" She held out her tray, but Dylan just stared at her, then burst out laughing.

"I'm a good lip reader, but not *that* good," he told her. "I have no idea what you just said!"

"Yeah, well, I have no idea what this *is*," she admitted, smiling back at him.

"You looked great on the big screen," he said.

"Don't remind me," Yasmin replied. "*So* embarrassing."

"Don't let her get to you," Dylan insisted. "I mean, consider the source."

He leaned toward her for a kiss, but Meredith stomped up and shouted, "Yasmin, that is *not* what I'm paying you for! No fraternizing with my guests! Get back to work!"

Meredith turned on her heel and heard a huge clatter from the other side of the yard. She whirled to see Cloe and Cameron facing each other, a spilled platter of food between them. Meredith climbed back onto the elephant to get a better view, and her lumbering ride gently knocked tables and chairs aside on his way to Meredith's destination, scattering party guests on all sides.

"Ugh, could you *be* any slower?" Meredith complained to the elephant. When they finally reached Cloe and Cameron, she glared down at both of them.

"If it isn't Cloe the Klutzy Clown," she shouted, staring at the spilled pile of food. "That's it, you're fired! Now clean up this disgusting mess before my guests see it."

Cloe bent down to pick up the food, and Cameron squatted down to help her. "Cameron, what are you doing?" Meredith demanded. "Leave that to the help!" But Cameron ignored her and finished helping Cloe clean up.

When he stood up, Meredith snapped, "Cameron, get me a drink." But he just stared at her, shook his head, and walked away. "Get back here, Cameron!" she yelled. "You do not just walk away from me like that!" She tried to slide off the elephant to chase after her boyfriend, but in her fury, she misjudged her distance from the ground and tumbled head over heels, directly into her seven-tier birthday cake. She skidded to a stop inches from the edge of her swimming pool, and her dog ran over and started licking icing from her face.

Everyone had stopped partying to watch Meredith's meltdown, and suddenly all her party guests were mingling, gossiping eagerly without any concern for clique divisions. Meredith stood up, swiping chunks of cake off her face, and surveyed the scene.

"Stop it!" she shouted. "This is *my* party, and this is *not* how it's supposed to go! Everyone get back to your assigned tables, right *now!*" But before she could say another word, she slid on a mound of frosting that had spattered on the ground, and grabbed at Avery and Quinn to break her fall, pushing them into the pool instead.

As they bobbed to the surface, the elephant turned and smacked Meredith with his trunk, knocking her into the pool with her friends.

When she resurfaced, she immediately spotted Cloe, Jade, Sasha and Yasmin peering down at her. "You! You've ruined *everything!*"

"Are you okay, Meredith?" Yasmin asked, stepping forward.

"I'll go get you a towel," Cloe offered, but Meredith stopped her.

"Look at what you've done to me!" she wailed. "There was going to be a cake and dancing and a whole circus performance, but now the party is *over!* You've destroyed my birthday. You've wrecked my life. You—you—you *brats!*" The girls just shrugged.

"I guess she doesn't want a towel," Sasha said as they rejoined the rest of the party.

Chapter 8

Yasmin stood at the front of the deserted music room, singing softly and beautifully into a microphone.

Dylan walked into the room and stopped short when he saw Yasmin, then headed for the speaker and put his hand on it so he could catch the vibrations of her voice. "Wow," he said when she finished her song. "Your singing is amazing."

Yasmin jumped at his voice. "You really think so?"

"Yeah," he told her. "Like, beyond amazing."

"Seriously?" Yasmin asked. "Thank you.

But ... how could you ..."

"Hear?" Dylan grinned at her. "It's okay, you can say it. It's true, I can't hear. But I heard you. Here, I'll show you."

Dylan turned on the stereo, then took Yasmin's hand and placed it on a speaker so she could feel the sound coursing through her.

She looked into Dylan's eyes, and smiled. "Whoa. That's how you could hear me?"

"So I didn't exactly hear your voice," Dylan admitted. "I felt your voice—and it felt amazing. You have a serious gift. You did sign up for the talent show, didn't you? Because you'll definitely win."

Yasmin took a step back. "Thanks, but no thanks. I can't sing in front of people. I literally get ill. It's not pretty."

Dylan laughed, then added, "Look, I can't hear, but I've learned to spin. Basically, you can do anything if you really want to. Seriously, it would be a crime to keep that voice to yourself. How about this—if I do the talent show, will you do it too?"

Yasmin looked down, afraid to meet his gaze. He took her hand and made a quick hand motion in sign language.

"What does that mean?" she asked.

"It means, 'Go for it,'" Dylan replied, and they shared a smile.

*   *   *

Dylan joined Yasmin and her friends for lunch that day, and as soon as he mentioned his talent show idea, Jade and Sasha couldn't stop talking about it. "You have to do it," Sasha insisted. "Meredith needs to be taken down, and you're the only one who can do it."

"Maybe so," Yasmin replied. "But there's no way I'm doing the talent show. You saw me freeze onstage at the party. I'm not exactly ready for a repeat performance."

"What if you sing while I spin?" Dylan offered.

"Hmm, let me think about it ... nope!" Yasmin told him.

"Come on," Sasha protested. "We'll all do it with you. You can sing, I'll choreograph,

Cloe can whip up an awesome video backdrop, and Jade will handle costumes!"

"Done!" Jade agreed.

"We'll need backup singers, too," Dylan added.

"And dancers!" Sasha exclaimed.

"Why stop there?" Jade asked. "We should get everyone who Meredith ever shot down to perform with us!"

"Perfect," Yasmin declared. "Since that's pretty much the entire population of Carry Nation High, then you definitely don't need to drag me onstage too."

"Listen, this year's winner gets a college scholarship," Jade continued. "Know anyone who might need one?"

"Cloe," Yasmin said thoughtfully. "I'd love to help, but I just can't do it."

"Why not?" Sasha demanded.

Yasmin smiled slyly. "Because, our act doesn't have a name yet!"

Cloe strolled up and teased, "Well, well, well, if it isn't the Brats."

Her friends exchanged looks, and Yasmin

cried, "Cloe, you're a genius!"

"I am?" Cloe asked, confused.

"I think you just named our talent show act," Yasmin explained. "What do you say, ladies? Should we call ourselves, 'The Brats'?"

"Totally!" her three best friends agreed.

That afternoon the girls leapt into action. They approached the marching band and gave them sheet music to one of Yasmin's songs. Jade got her entire Home-Ec class to help make costumes for their performance. Cloe hung out in the AV room with a bunch of AV geeks, cutting together footage that she'd shot with a school video camera, and Sasha taught her best friends and her cheerleading squad a bunch of amazing dance moves.

In the Home-Ec room, Jade was just putting the finishing touches on a "Brats" warm-up jacket when she stepped back and looked at the letters laid out on the back. "It's not quite right," she muttered. She stared at her handiwork for a moment, then exclaimed, "I've got it!" She grabbed a "z" instead of an "s" and spelled out "Bratz."

"Way hipper!" she exclaimed as she ironed the letters on.

The girls took over the Carry Nation auditorium to practice their act, where Sasha ran them through their dance number every day after school. "Five, six, seven, eight!" she shouted, and the girls launched into their routine. She kept running them through it until they all finally collapsed on the floor, panting.

"You're killing us!" Jade cried.

"Soccer practice started like half an hour ago," Cloe complained.

"So did science club," Jade added.

"I know ... so did cheerleading," Sasha told them. "And girl, right now I couldn't bring it even if it was already here."

"Come on, you guys," Yasmin exclaimed, hopping up excitedly. "If we're gonna be in this talent show, we have to make sure we look, oh, I dunno—talented?"

The girls slowly pulled themselves off the floor and ran through their routine again, not noticing Avery, offstage, filming everything.

Sasha stumbled through her front door that night, and her dad looked up, surprised. "Hey, honey. Aren't you supposed to be at your mom's tonight?"

Sasha looked around and realized that in her exhaustion, she'd gone to the wrong house. "Can you just call her and see if it's okay for me to stay here tonight?" Her dad held the phone out toward her, but Sasha shook her head. "Can't you just talk to her?"

"You know, I'm really proud of how hard you're working," her dad told her. "And I'm so glad you and your friends were able to look past your differences and make up."

"Thanks, Dad," Sasha replied. "Maybe one day you and Mom will do the same thing." She trudged off to her bedroom as her dad stared after her.

"Maybe," he murmured.

Meanwhile, Cloe wandered into the kitchen of her apartment, on the brink of total collapse. She grabbed a bottle of water from the refrigerator and chugged it, not noticing her mom watching her until she had finished the entire bottle.

"Your soccer coach called," Katie said. "You've been missing practice."

"As soon as this show is over, I'll be back on track with soccer, I swear," Cloe replied.

"Cloe, your coach is talking about cutting you from the team," Katie explained. "And if you get cut, there goes your college scholarship. And no scholarship—"

"Means no college," Cloe sighed.

"I'm so sorry, Sweetie," Katie told her daughter as Cloe wandered out of the room, headed for bed.

*   *   *

The next day in the Carry Nation security booth, Avery showed her friend the footage she'd shot of the Bratz. "No way," she declared. "They ruined my Super Sweet Sixteen. I'm not going to let them ruin my talent show."

She picked up her cell phone and dialed Yasmin's number. "Yasmin, it's Meredith. I'm calling with some bad news. Meet me in the security booth in an hour."

When Yasmin arrived, Meredith explained, "It's really in your best interest to drop out of the talent show. Otherwise, I'll have to reveal the truth about Clover and her pathetic mom."

"That's Cloe," Yasmin corrected her.

"Same thing," Meredith continued. "Either way, I'm pretty sure she wouldn't want the whole school to know that her mom used to be my maid, and that she got fired when little *Cloe* stole my favorite doll."

"You are so devious," Yasmin told her.

"*Thank* you!" Meredith replied. "I hate to do it, but you can certainly see my predicament—and yours."

"You're pathetic," Yasmin declared. "You spend half your time documenting dirt on everyone else. You really should get a life."

"Oh, I have one," Meredith said. "And it's *fabulous!* You see, Yazzie, this is just the way life works. In order for there to be winners, there must be losers ... and that's where you come in."

"Save it," Yasmin snapped. "Just leave Cloe alone, okay?"

Yasmin dashed from the booth into the auditorium, where her friends were rehearsing.

"Better late than never!" Sasha called when she spotted Yasmin.

"Guys, I'm dropping out of the show," Yasmin announced. "I tried, but I just can't do it."

"What?!" Jade, Cloe, and Sasha cried.

"You're joking, right?" Sasha asked.

"No, I'm not," Yasmin replied. "Look, you guys pushed me into this, and it's just not my thing."

"It's not *your* thing?" Cloe demanded. "I'm about to get kicked off the soccer team so I can help you win this talent show, and *you're* the one quitting?"

"Sorry," Yasmin said, not meeting her friends' eyes, "but I don't want to talk about it."

"You don't want to talk about it?" Jade shouted. "What about the fact that my grades have dropped because of all these rehearsals? Can we talk about that?"

"Chill, Jade," Yasmin told her. "It's not that big of a deal."

"What happened to sticking together?" Sasha asked. "What happened to best friends forever?"

"I guess I'm just not feeling it anymore," Yasmin said.

"Well, that's just great, Yasmin," Jade snapped. "Do me a favor, okay? Delete me from your contacts."

"Me too," Cloe added.

"Same here," Sasha agreed.

"Sure," Yasmin replied. "I will." She walked away and hurried straight home, where she collapsed on her bed and burst into tears.

Her grandma heard her and came into Yasmin's room, sitting down beside her and stroking her hair. "I was just trying to protect my friends," she sobbed. "But I lost them instead."

"Then tell them that," Bubbie suggested. "Give your friends a chance to *be* friends. You owe them that much."

Chapter 9

The night of the talent show, Cloe, Jade and Sasha lounged around Cloe's bedroom, munching morosely on a plateful of cookies. Cloe's mom rapped lightly on the door-frame before strolling in to join them.

"Are you girls almost ready for the talent show?" Katie asked.

"We're not going, Mom," Cloe replied.

"What?" Katie cried. "Why not?"

"Yasmin bailed on us," Cloe explained. "She just quit, out of nowhere."

"I just can't believe she would do this," Sasha added.

"I can't believe it either," Katie told them. "In fact, I *don't* believe it. I mean, maybe there's something going on here that you don't know about."

"Doubt it," Sasha sighed.

"Come on, girls," Katie protested. "Has Yasmin ever, in her entire life, done anything to hurt you guys?"

The girls looked at each other. "No," they all admitted in unison.

"So don't you think you owe it to your friend to dig a little deeper, maybe figure out why she's doing this?" Katie insisted.

Cloe, Jade and Sasha exchanged glances, then nodded and headed for the door.

Back at her place, Yasmin sat staring at her phone. Taking a deep breath, she dialed Sasha's cell phone number. "Sasha, I need to talk to you guys," Yasmin said. "Like, face to face."

"Okay," Sasha agreed instantly.

"Okay?" Yasmin asked.

"Yeah. Look out your window, Yas," Sasha

told her. Yasmin hurried to the window and pushed the curtains aside. Outside, her three best friends stood on the lawn, waving up at her. She tossed her phone on the bed and raced downstairs to join them.

"We should have known you were just protecting us," Cloe said.

"But I didn't tell you," Yasmin replied.

"Yeah, but we should have known anyway," Cloe insisted. "We're best friends forever, no matter what."

"And we still want to do the talent show with you," Jade added.

"But Cloe, Meredith has awful ..."

Yasmin began, but Cloe interrupted.

"What*ever*! If we let Meredith scare us into quitting this show, then she's in control again," Cloe replied. "We have to stick together and stand up to her, once and for all. Are you in, Yasmin?"

"Sure," Yasmin agreed. "We better get over there. But first, I have one stop to make."

"Yas, we don't want to miss our chance to crush Meredith once and for all," Cloe protested.

"Oh, we won't!" Katie exclaimed, hopping out of her van. "Get in, girls—I'll get you there!" Yasmin called out directions from the back of the van as they sped over to Dylan's house, while the girls all hurriedly changed into the costumes Jade had made.

When Katie pulled to a stop, Yasmin ran up to the front door and pounded on it until Dylan's mom answered.

"Um, hi," Yasmin said shyly. "Is Dylan home?"

He appeared in the hallway behind his mom and demanded, "What are you doing here?"

"I'll leave you two alone," his mom interjected, heading for her bedroom.

Yasmin took a step toward Dylan and explained, "We're doing the talent show and I ... we ... want you with us."

Dylan's eyes widened in excitement, but

he said, "Are you sure? You don't have to, you know."

"I've never been more sure about anything in my life!" she declared.

Dylan leaned in and gave her a quick kiss, then grabbed her hand and cried, "Come on, let's go!"

Katie screeched to a stop in front of the high school and they all ran inside, just in time to hear the announcer declare, "Ladies and gentlemen, live from Carry Nation High School, it's Meredith and the Meredettes!"

Meredith, in a diamond-studded gown, burst through a pair of ostrich feather fans held up by Avery and Quinn and launched into a dazzling song. While she sang, The Bratz and Dylan scurried through the audience, tracking down everyone who had been a part of their act to tell them the show was still on.

"Thank you, thank you!" Meredith exclaimed, blowing kisses at the audience. "Now, for the moment I've been waiting for—I'm just kidding! The moment we've *all* been waiting for! Let's see who you have chosen as this year's most talented student at Carry Nation High. Judges, the envelope, please."

But just then, Yasmin ran onstage. "Wait a minute."

The spotlight turned to Yasmin as she continued, "There's one more act."

"Um, no, there's not," Meredith declared. "The show is over."

Sasha's dad stood up in the audience and called, "Now, listen. The girls signed up and they have a right to perform."

Sasha's mom stood up beside him and shouted, "He's right!"

"Uh, I think I know the rules, and the fact is, they already *un*signed up," Meredith snapped.

"Hey!" Sasha yelled. "Don't talk to my parents like that!"

"Meredith, it's over," Jade told her. "Cloe, introduce us."

The audience fell silent as Cloe stepped up to the microphone. "Ladies and gentlemen—I give you, The Bratz!"

"Wait!" Meredith wailed. She turned to Yasmin and demanded, "Are you sure you want to do this?" Yasmin looked at her friends and they all nodded determinedly.

"Well, then, I guess you leave me no choice," Meredith announced, snatching the mic away from Cloe. "I didn't want to do this, but as your Student Body President, it's my duty to keep you informed of all important matters. That's why I am obligated to tell you who these brats *really* are. Avery?"

Up in the control booth, Avery hooked up Meredith's jump drive, and an image of Jade appeared on the huge screens behind the Meredith. "Exhibit A: The Fashionista. Or is she?" As Avery clicked through several shots of Jade in her cool threads, Meredith continued, "This is who you think she is. But *this* is who she really is." Avery clicked again in the control booth, and a photo of Jade in her parent-approved plaid skirt and sweater set popped onscreen. The audience gasped, and Jade's parents looked shocked.

Jade hurried onstage and replied, "Look, here's the truth. I'm not either of those girls you saw up there. I love science and math and my parents. A lot. But I also have a passion for fashion, and it's how I express who I am. I just want to be accepted for everything that I am—not just one side of me."

She looked at her parents apologetically, but they smiled back at her. Her dad even hopped up from his front-row seat to snap a picture of his daughter.

"Okay, what about this?" Meredith demanded, pointing to Cloe. "Soccer jock, all-American girl, perfect daughter? You decide. When her mother desperately needed a job, my family was kind enough to offer her employment … as our maid.

But how did her daughter repay this kindness? By stealing my favorite dolly. And when she wouldn't admit it, we had no choice but to fire her mother."

"My mother did clean Meredith's house," Cloe admitted. "She would do anything to provide for us. My mom is my hero." Katie beamed from the audience as Cloe added, "But I did *not* take your doll. I may be poor, but I'm no thief."

Cherish jumped up in the audience and yelled, "Actually, I took it!" As her sister turned to glare at her, Cherish explained, "You were using it as a doorstop, Meredith. I had to rescue it from you."

"As long as we're confessing, I have something to say," Manny announced, leaping up beside Cherish. "I eavesdropped on my sister and then I betrayed her. And I'm really, really sorry."

"Well, that's all very interesting," Meredith interrupted, "but we still need to announce a winner. So …"

But just then, Mr. Whitman strode onto the stage. "Actually, there's something I need to confess too. See, I love being a music teacher, but I have another outlet for my music. You know me as Mr. Whitman. But to the rest of the world, I'm …" He pulled off his glasses, ruffled his hair, and struck a cool pose.

"DJ Wax?!" the audience cried.

Mr. Whitman pointed to Dylan, who started spinning.

Yasmin grabbed the microphone and declared, "Meredith, this one's for you!" She and her friends started singing, and they sounded totally amazing. Soon most of the school was onstage—the marching band, dancers, gymnasts, choir, and cheerleaders, all doing their part to make the Bratz show utterly spectacular. A video screen dropped down to show Cloe's footage of the school year.

Cameron started to head for the stage and Meredith clutched his hand. "If you go up on that stage, I'm never speaking to you again."

"That's the best offer I've had all day," he replied, and joined Cloe onstage, dancing beside her.

When they finished the song, The Bratz got a standing ovation. Yasmin's best friends surrounded her in a group hug, while the other kids onstage all jumped up and down, cheering.

But then Principal Dimly stomped onto the stage and shouted, "Attention everyone!" The crowd quieted down, and he announced, "The winner of this year's talent show is…" He opened the envelope slowly. "It looks like we have a tie! Well, that's a first. I guess there's only one way to settle this fairly. I would like to present this year's Golden Hatchet to … Meredith Baxter Dimly!"

Principal Dimly handed his daughter the trophy, and she squealed, "I won! I won! Look everyone, I won!" The audience applauded half-heartedly.

"But, in the spirit of harmony, I would like to award the scholarship to our runners-up, The Bratz," Principal Dimly continued, and the crowd burst into cheers.

"Daddy, what are you doing?" Meredith wailed.

"It's not like we need the money, honey," he explained. "Anyway, you won the trophy—that's the *real* first prize."

"Yay, so now I have four," Meredith complained. "Whoopdidoo."

"Stop whining, Meredith!" her father snapped, standing up to her for the first time. "You tied for first place in a very competitive field. Isn't that enough for you?"

Yasmin strolled up and interrupted the family feud. "Meredith, you're really talented. Great job!"

"Thank you," Meredith replied sweetly. "You know, it's true that the cream always rises to the top." Sasha was fuming, but before she could say a word, a man in a business suit rushed onto the stage. "Meredith, Tom McShavie, vice president of MTV networks," he said, shaking Meredith's hand. "Great show. You know, I caught you're my Super Sweet Sixteen episode, and it got the best numbers to date. You in the pool … outrageous!"

"My idea," Meredith informed him.

"Smart girl," he replied. Then he spotted The Bratz and dropped Meredith's hand. "But you four girls—wow! You've got superstar written all over you!"

"We do?" the four best friends gasped.

"Without question," Tom told them. "Hey, we've got a movie premiere next Saturday night. How would you girls like to perform on the red carpet?"

"I think we could do that," Sasha agreed, grinning.

"Fantastic," Tom replied. "We'll be in touch."

"Hey, what about me?" Meredith complained.

The MTV executive shook his head and chuckled. "That swimming pool gag—priceless!" he said before walking away.

Cloe, Jade, Sasha and Yasmin stared at each other in amazement, then started jumping up and down, squealing with excitement.

"What did I do to deserve this?" Meredith moaned.

"Oh my gosh, a red carpet performance!" Sasha exclaimed.

"But we have even more exciting news than that," Jade pointed out.

"What's more exciting than the red carpet?" Cloe cried.

"That scholarship money," Yasmin explained. "Cloe, we decided that if we won, the scholarship was going to you! Now you can go to film school, or whatever you want!"

"Oh my gosh, I love you guys!" Cloe cried. "But are you sure?"

"Absolutely," Sasha agreed.

"Positively," Jade added.

"Because after all, that's what best friends forever are for!" Yasmin declared.